Judy Moody & Stink

THE HOLLY JOLIDAY

Megan McDonald

illustrated by Peter H. Reynolds

W
BOOKS

First published 2008 by Walker Books Ltd
87 Vauxhall Walk, London SE11 5HJ

2 4 6 8 10 9 7 5 3

Text © 2007 Megan McDonald
Illustrations © 2007 Peter H. Reynolds
Judy Moody font © 2004 Peter H. Reynolds

British Library Cataloguing
in Publication Data
a catalogue record for this book
is available from the British Library

ISBN 978-1-4063-1365-9

www.walkerbooks.co.uk

Judy Moody & Stink

THE HOLLY JOLIDAY

**Books by Megan McDonald
and Peter H. Reynolds**
Judy Moody
Judy Moody Gets Famous!
Judy Moody Saves the World!
Judy Moody Predicts the Future
Doctor Judy Moody
Judy Moody Declares Independence!
Judy Moody Around the World in 8 1/2 Days
The Judy Moody Journal
*The Judy Moody Double-Rare Way-Not Boring
Book of Fun Stuff to Do*
Stink: The Incredible Shrinking Kid
Stink and the Incredible Super-Galactic Jawbreaker
Stink and the World's Worst Super-Stinky Sneakers

Books by Megan McDonald
Ant and Honey Bee: What a Pair!

Books by Peter H. Reynolds
The Dot
Ish
So Few of Me

www.judymoody.co.uk   www.stinkmoody.com

For my family
M. M.

To the family who knows how to celebrate
year-round – the Doucettes of Dedham, Mass...
Bill, Cheryl, Alex and Ian!
P. H. R.

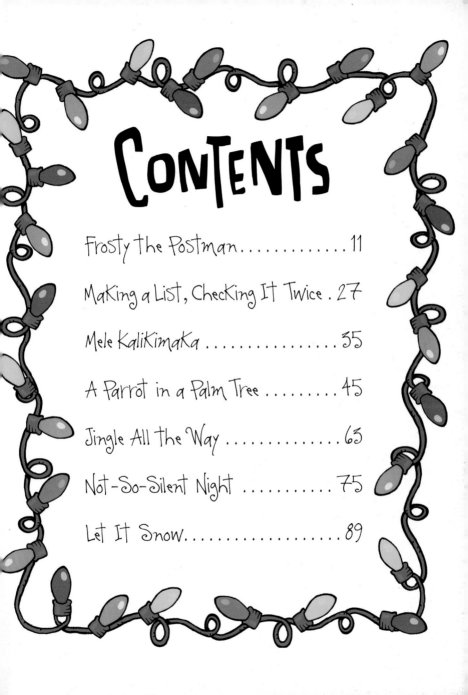

CONTENTS

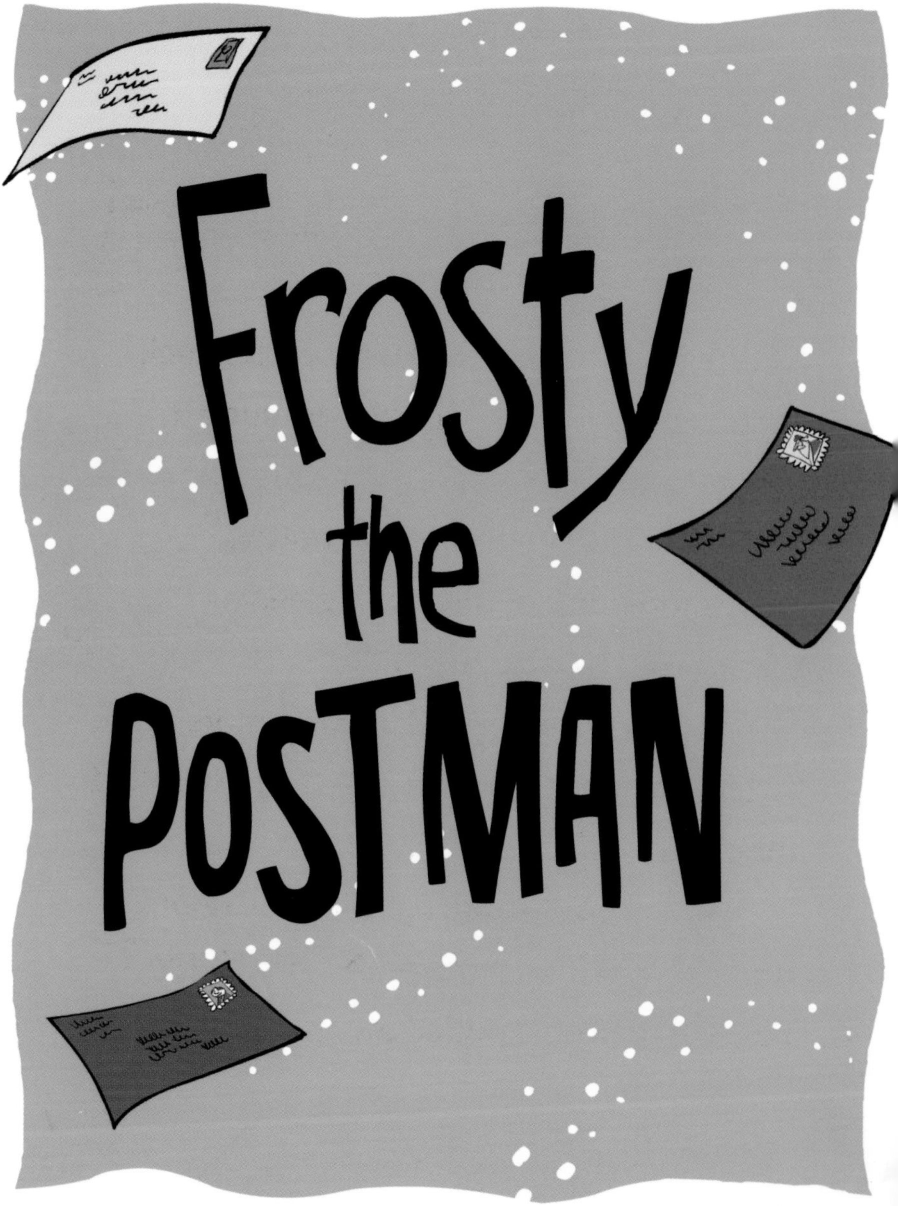
Frosty
the
POSTMAN

Stink was glued to the weather channel, when out on the porch he heard such a clatter! *Thunk! Clunk!* Stink sprang from the sofa to see what was the matter. "Postman!" he shouted with glee. "Somebody's got a parcel!"

"Stink, I hope you didn't write more letters and order more free stuff," Judy called after him. "Mum and Dad will be mad."

"Nope," said Stink, opening the door and running down the path to catch the post van before it pulled away. He liked talking to Mr Harvey, the postman. Mr Harvey had a ponytail and a dog named Pork Chop.

"How's Pork Chop?" Stink asked, but when the postman turned around, it wasn't the postman at all. He did not have a ponytail. And he did not look like someone who had a dog named Pork Chop.

This guy had white fuzzy hair and smiley wrinkles. He had a white bushy beard and hairy eyebrows, and he wore a furry hat with the earflaps turned up. He did not look like a postman.

"Who are you?" asked Stink. "And where's Mr Harvey?"

"I'm the new guy," said the not-postman. "Glad to meet you. My name's Frost. Call me Jack." He grinned and winked and raised his bushy white eyebrows.

"No way! You mean *you're* Jack Frost? For real? Like the snowman? Like the guy who paints frosty pictures on leaves and windows?"

"That's me," Jack said. "And guess what happens when a dog bites me?"

"What?" Stink asked.

"I get *Frost* bite," he said, grinning. Stink howled over that one.

Jack Frost handed Stink two more boxes. "Special delivery today. These didn't fit through your letter box."

"Are any from the North Pole?" Stink shook the boxes. One was from the L. L. Beanery and smelled like coffee. The other one was as heavy as books but sounded like … fruitcake! Sick!

"Probably just fruitcake," said Stink. "My grandma Lou sends us one every year around Christmas. Our cat, Mouse, is the only one who eats it!"

"Better luck next time, huh?" Jack said.

"Hey, if you're Jack Frost," said Stink, "I was wondering … do you think you could deliver snow this year? All I want for Christmas is snow."

"Snow, huh? Well, you never know. Might be able to arrange it for you this year."

"You can do that?" Stink asked. "For real?"

Jack Frost laughed and tugged at his white beard, winking and looking up at the sky. "From what I can tell, there's a low-pressure system moving in. Cold front could get here as early as this weekend."

"Wow!" said Stink. "So you can predict the weather too?"

"I've been in this line of work for a long time. I can feel the weather in my bones." Jack Frost stuck out his tongue. "Right now, I can almost taste snow in the air."

"I have a super-good sniffer," said Stink. "Maybe I can smell it in the air." He closed his eyes and stuck his nose in the air. *Sniff,*

sniff. He pictured catching snowflakes on his tongue. *Sniff, sniff.* He pictured a snowball fight. *Sniff, sniff.* He pictured a great big whopping whiteout. "Yep, I think I smell snow," said Stink.

Stink and Jack Frost were quiet for a minute. Together they looked up at the gloomy grey sky and sniffed the moist, damp air.

"My big sister says it never snows in Virginia," said Stink. "My big sister says there's too much global warming. My big sister says there's like a billion-to-one chance of snow this year."

"Your big sister sounds pretty clever, huh?"

17

"She thinks so," said Stink.

"It could happen," said Jack Frost. "One winter, back in 1980, we got thirty-five centimetres in one day. Broke all the records."

"Whoa!" said Stink.

"See? You just might get your fluffy stuff after all," said Jack Frost. "Think *snow*. Feel it in your bones."

"Thanks!" said Stink. "It's lucky I ran into you – you know, to put in my order and everything."

"Well, I'm not making any promises," Jack Frost said with a wink, "but I'll keep my fingers crossed!"

"Cool yule!" said Stink.

∴ ✳ • ✳ ∙ ✳ ∙.

Stink came back inside singing, *"Frosty the postman was a jolly, happy soul...* Wow! You're never gonna believe... Guess who I just met!"

"Mr Harvey, the postman?" said Judy, looking up from her list.

"Nope. Who's got a beard that's long and white?"

"Must be Santa."

"Wrong again. Jack Frost. I just talked to Jack Frost! No lie!"

"Really? Was the Sandman out there too? How about the Tooth Fairy?" Judy laughed herself silly.

"Hardee-har-har. That's his real name," said Stink. "Ask him."

"Our postman's name is Mr Harvey," said Judy.

"Not any more. There was a new guy out there. Mr Frost. As in Jack. As in Jack Frost. He knows all about snow and everything. And he says I might get snow for Christmas."

"Stink, I hate to break it to you, but Jack Frost is invisible. Or as tiny as an elf or something."

"Or something," said Stink.

"First of all," said Judy, counting off on her fingers, "you can't just see him. Jack Frost sneaks around at night or way early in the morning to make frost on windows and leaves."

"That's what I used to think!" said Stink.

"Second, Jack Frost is NOT a postman. I mean, what are the chances?"

"Lots of people have more than one job," Stink said.

"Third, even if he is a postman, he wouldn't be in Virginia. He would be in Alaska or Minnesota—"

"I know! What are the chances that Mr Harvey would just disappear and Jack Frost would show up, right here on Croaker Road, this time of year? But did you ever think maybe that's why he's here – 'cos it's *our* turn to have snow? I'm telling you –

he can smell it coming. His bones told him too."

"So this Jack Frost character also has talking bones?"

"Yeah, and he said it would be no pressure to bring snow. Or low pressure. I forget."

"Stink, believe me, it hasn't snowed here for like a million years."

"Not true!" said Stink. "Jack Frost said that one winter it snowed thirty-five centimetres here in one day!"

"When was this?" asked Judy.

"Back in 1980."

"OK, so *half* a million years. Stink, I'm telling you—"

"You're not the weatherman," Stink told Judy.

"Neither is Jack Frost. He's the *post*man, Stink." Judy let out a little puff of air. "Wait – now you have me believing this stuff."

Making a List, Checking It Twice

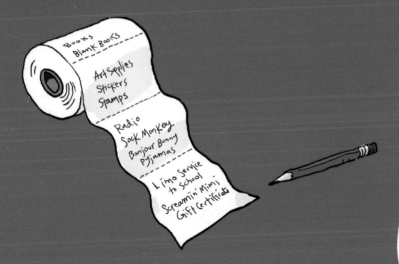

Books
Blank Books

Art Supplies
Stickers
Stamps

Radio
Sock Monkey
Bonjour Bunny
Pyjamas

Limo Service
to School
Screamin' Mimi's
Gift Certificate

Stickers
Stamps

Radio
Sock Monkey
Bonjour Bunny
Pyjamas

Limo Service
to School
Screamin' Mimi
Gift Certificate

Judy Moody went back to making a list and checking it twice. Not a think-up-nicknames-for-Stink list. Not a things-to-do-when-you're-home-sick list.

A T.P. (not Toad Pee) list. A toilet-paper list of all the stuff she wanted to get for Christmas. A *Totally Presents* list.

It wasn't easy writing on toilet paper. But T.P. was the only thing long enough to fit all the presents she wanted.

Judy unrolled her T.P. list. It went out the door and onto the landing and past

Books
Blank Books
Art Supplies
Stickers
Stamps

 27

Stink's room and down the stairs. It rolled right across the *S* encyclopedia Stink was reading for the one-hundredth time.

"Hey!" yelled Stink.

"Sorry," said Judy. "Just making my list."

"This is like ten miles long!" said Stink.

"So? That means I get ten miles of presents," said Judy.

Stink went back to his encyclopedia. He was reading about snowy owls and snowshoe hares. He was reading about snowdrop trees. He was reading about Snowflake Bentley.

Judy didn't get it. Usually Stink wanted tons and tons of stuff. Piles more stuff than Judy. *Miles* more stuff than Judy.

"Stink, you'd better make a list," Judy told him. "Only five more days till Christmas."

"I already have a list," said Stink.

"Where is it?" Judy asked.

"In my head."

"You'd better write it down, Stinkerbell."

"I'll remember."

"How are you going to remember? If you don't write it down, how will I know what to get you? How will Mum and Dad know? And Grandma Lou? And Webster and Sophie of the Elves and any real elves?"

"Fine. I'll write it down." Stink tore a blank page from his notebook. He scribbled something in two seconds, then put his pencil down.

"Done!" said Stink.

"Done?" asked Judy. "How can you be done already? I've been working on my list for three hundred and sixty-something days!"

Judy picked up the piece of paper. Stink had printed just one puny word. That one word was *snow.*

"That's it? Just one thing? Snow? That's not even a present."

"That's all I want."

"Not even snow boots or a snow hat or snowshoes or a snowboard?"

"Nope."

"Not even an inflatable igloo with fake snowballs?"

"Nope."

"Not even a snow-globe kit or an arctic blast jet sled?"

"Actually, an arctic blast jet sled would be cool. But no. All I really want is snow."

"Stink, that is so way boring!"

"Boring? Are you mad? What about snowmen and snow forts and snow angels and snowball fights? What about sledging? And what about snow days off from school?"

"Have you looked outside lately? Hel-lo! The postman was wearing shorts the other day. And I saw a robin yesterday."

"What a grinch," said Stink.

"Stink, I told you it hardly ever even snows in Virginia. What are the chances it'll snow *this* year? For real?"

"It better snow," said Stink, "or I'm moving to Vermont."

Mele Kalikimaka

"Last day of school before Christmas!" Judy shouted when she got home from school. Judy and Stink dumped their backpacks on the sofa.

"So, what did you do on your last day?" asked Mum.

"Ate candy canes," said Stink.

"We had an *Aloha* Christmas party," said Judy. "Like in Hawaii."

"Sophie of the Elves was my Secret Santa," said Stink.

"We drank pink flamingo punch and

played Pin the Monkey on the Palm Tree."

"And I got a snow globe all the way from Vermont!" said Stink.

"Mr Todd wore sunglasses and a Hawaiian shirt and gave everybody a *lei* to wear tonight," said Judy, pointing to her flower necklace. "Don't forget that tonight is the Tenth Annual Holly Jolly Holiday Happening at school."

"We made a field guide to snowflakes," said Stink, digging into his backpack and pulling out a chart with shapes. "Even though no two are exactly the same, a lot of snowflakes have the same basic shapes to start with. Stellar dendrites are like trees, but lots of other snowflakes have shapes like pencils, prisms, plates and pompoms."

"We learned that *Mele Kalikimaka* means Merry Christmas in Hawaiian."

"We heard this story about a famous guy who worked out how to take pictures of thousands of snowflakes."

"Was his name Jack Frost?" asked Judy.

"Snowflake Bentley," said Stink. "He's in the encyclopedia. Two times. Under *S* and under *B* too."

"In Hawaii, my name would be I-U-K-I."

"I Yucky!" said Stink. "That's the perfect name for you."

"Ho, ho, ho, Stink. You say it *Ee-oo-kee*. Your name's K-I-M-O, pronounced *Kee-mo*. I asked Mr Todd."

"Sounds like Kimo and Iuki both had an exciting day," said Mum. "Are you both ready for the Christmas show tonight?"

"YES!" said Judy. "My class is singing 'The Twelve Days of Christmas in Hawaii'! Rare!"

"How about you, Stink? Did your class practise the play of 'The Night Before Christmas'?"

"Don't remind me," said Stink. "I have to be a mouse again. Sophie of the Elves gets to be a sugarplum fairy. Webster gets to be Prancer or Vixen – I forget which. But no, I have to be a shorty-pants mouse. Every year!"

"You could wear *long* pants," Judy suggested.

"At least you have a mouse costume already," said Mum.

"Yeah, put it on and give us a sneak peek. I mean a *squeak* peek." Judy cracked herself up.

"Hardee-har-har. I wish just once I could be something like … a stellar dendrite," Stink said wistfully.

"Stellar dandruff! Stink, there's no stellar dandruff in 'The Night Before Christmas'," Judy teased.

Stink went upstairs to try on his mouse costume.

"And a par-rot in a palm tree." Judy practised singing while she fed Jaws. *"And a par-rot in a palm tree."* Judy practised

singing while she put a jingle-bell collar on Mouse. *"And a par-rot in a palm tree."* Judy practised singing while she laid the table.

Where was Stink? Why was it taking him about a hundred million years just to put on mouse ears?

Finally, Stink came downstairs, covering his not-mouse ears. "I thought there were *twelve* days of Christmas. What happened to the other eleven?"

"Ho, ho, ho," said Judy. She looked at what Stink was wearing. "Hey, where's your mouse costume? How come you're wearing all white? I thought mice were brown."

"A mouse can be white," said Stink.

"Yeah, maybe a science mouse. Like the kind that gets tests done on him. Or runs through mazes. Or gets eaten by snakes. Not a Night-Before-Christmas mouse."

"A white mouse goes with a white Christmas," said Stink.

"Not a creature was stirring, not even a science mouse!" Judy roared.

When the Moodys got to Virginia Dare School that night, the hall was decorated with evergreen branches, pinecone wreaths and candy canes. Blinking white lights twinkled round the doorway.

"The school looks so pretty tonight," said Mum.

"They did a great job," Dad agreed.

"It would look better with snow," said Stink.

"Wait till you see the decorations for our song," Judy told her parents. "The whole stage is going to be decked out like Hawaii. And Frank's bringing in Cookie, his real-live parrot. Cookie talks and everything!"

"Better go and find your classes, you two," said Mum.

"Break a leg," said Dad.

"Look for me!" said Stink. "At the beginning of 'The Night Before Christmas'."

"Stink, I mean Kimo, it's going to be pretty hard to miss a science mouse in the middle of a Christmas celebration," said Judy.

∴ ✳ • ✳ ∴ ✳ ∴

The lights went down, and the Tenth Annual Holly Jolly Holiday Happening began. Ms Tuxedo, the principal, welcomed everyone, and the music teacher played "Let It Snow" softly in the background.

First up was the nursery class singing the Kwanzaa Spelling Song. The fifth grade played a jazzy version of "Feliz Navidad". The first grade recited a Hanukkah poem about eight little candles. The fourth grade acted out a short play about *Sinter Klaas* from Holland. Finally, it was time for Judy's class. Judy, Rocky and Frank stood stage left, beside Class 3T's blow-up plastic palm tree. A rainbow of pink, green and blue spotlights shone down on them. They were all wearing shorts, flip-flops and Hawaiian shirts.

Judy squinted in the bright light. She felt her hands sweat. She felt her neck itch under the plastic flower *lei*.

"Can you hold Cookie?" Frank asked Judy, holding out his real-live parrot. "I'm too nervous."

"I'm too nervous too," said Judy.

"The parrot has to sit up in the palm tree," said Rocky. "Like in the song. Hurry up! Mr Todd's about to start!"

Frank held out his arm. Cookie flapped her wings, hopping from Frank's arm onto the palm-tree prop.

"Tonight," Mr Todd announced, "we are celebrating Christmas traditions from all around the world. Class 3T chose to honour

Christmas in Hawaii with its very own
version of a well-known song."

Judy took a deep breath. Everyone sang:

"Number One Day of Christmas,
My tutu *gave to me*
A par-rot in a palm tree!"

Judy smiled and pushed the hair out
of her eyes.

"Number Two Day of Christmas,
My tutu *gave to me*
Two pink flamingoes
And a par-rot in a palm tree!"

"Mary had a lit-tle lamb!" sang Cookie.
The audience cracked up.

"Quiet, Cookie," Frank warned, shaking his finger at her.

*"Number Three Day of Christmas,
My tutu gave to me
Three boogie boards,
Two pink flamingoes,
And a par-rot in a palm tree!"*

"Mary had a lit-tle lamb!" sang Cookie, bobbing her head. The audience laughed even harder. For eleven whole verses, as soon as Class 3T sang *"parrot in a palm tree"*, Cookie squawked, *"Mary had a little lamb."*

*"Twelve ukuleles,
Eleven ice cubes melting,*

Ten fish a-leaping,
Nine hula dancers,
Eight Santas surfing,
Seven sharks a-swimming,
Six flip-flops flapping,
Five gol-den pineapples!
Four flower leis,
Three boogie boards,
Two pink flamingoes…
And a par-rot in a palm tree!"

Class 3T sang its heart out on the last verse. Just as the audience prepared to clap, Cookie sang out, *"Maria tenía un pequeño cordero!"* – "Mary had a little lamb" in Spanish! The audience went wild. They roared. They stood up and clapped. They yelled *encore*!

"Mele Kalikimaka!" shouted Class 3T, and they all took a bow before the curtains closed.

"Cookie! Bad girl!" said Frank behind the curtain. "Get down here. Right now!" He held out his arm.

"Lit-tle lamb!" sang Cookie, ruffling her feathers. But she would not come down out of the palm tree.

"All that practising and she ruined the show!" said Frank.

"No way!" said Judy. "Everybody loved it. Cookie was the star of the show."

"They think we planned it that way!" said Rocky.

"How does Cookie know 'Mary Had a Little Lamb' anyway?" asked Judy.

"She listens to Dog Cat Radio on the internet," said Frank. "My mum leaves it on to keep our pets company when we're not home, and they play animal songs all day. They have a Spanish hour too."

Mr Todd stepped into the spotlight once more. "Thank you, Cookie the parrot, for celebrating diversity with us tonight!" Cookie bobbed her head up and down, like she was taking a bow.

"And now, for our grand finale, the second-graders will perform 'The Night Before Christmas'."

"That's Stink's class," said Judy to Rocky and Frank. "Let's go and sit in the audience so we can watch. Mrs Dempster is reading the poem, and the kids are acting it out. Stink's the mouse. And his part's right near the beginning."

The lights went down. The audience grew quiet. The curtain opened.

"*'Twas the night before Christmas,*" read Mrs D. in a hushed voice. She was sitting in a big armchair at the front of the stage. A second-grader walked onstage, holding up a cardboard moon attached to a stick.

"*When all through the house…*" Mrs D. continued. Three more second-graders dragged a cardboard house onstage.

"Not a creature was stirring…" read Mrs D. *"Not even a mouse."*

The whole audience got super still. Not a mobile was sounding, not even a cough.

"Where's Stink?" Judy whispered. "That's his line."

"Not even a *mouse*," Mrs D. read again, a little louder.

"Oh, no!" Judy whispered. "Stink missed his cue!"

The audience fidgeted. Chairs squeaked. Feet shuffled.

"MOUSE!" Mrs D. said again, practically shouting this time.

"Where is he?" asked Judy. Before Mrs D. could say *mouse* again, someone –

or something – burst onstage in a flash
of white.

Frank Pearl leaned forward, trying to see.
"Is that Stink?"

"I thought you said he was a mouse,"
Rocky whispered.

"He is," said Judy. "A bright, white
science mouse!"

But when the spotlight found Stink,
he was not a science mouse. He was not
a mouse at all.

He was a snowflake! A bright, shiny
snowflake. Stink was dressed all in white,
and strapped to his back was a giant, six-
pointed sparkly snowflake. On his T-shirt,
in black letters, he'd written STELLAR DENDRITE.

"I can't look," said Judy, covering her face.

"Not a creature was stirring!" yelled Stink, whirling and twirling in the spotlight. "Not even a snowflake!"

It was clear from the look on her face that Mrs Dempster had not expected a blizzard. But after Stink floated around for a moment or two, she kept right on reading the poem, as if nothing strange had happened.

Judy had known Stink to be a mouse plenty of times. She had known him to be a human flag. She had known him to be James Madison, Shortest President Ever. But never in a million years had she dreamed that Stink would one day dance onstage as a stellar dendrite.

"What a flake," said Judy. "As in *snow*flake. Or should I say, snow *freak*?" Judy and Stink would be laughing like a bowl full of jelly over this one for many Christmases to come.

It was the night before Christmas, and all through the house, the Moodys were stirring, even Mouse. Dad was ordering Hawaiian pizza (with pineapple!), and Mum was wrapping presents. Stink was shaking presents as fast as Mum could wrap them, then tucking them under the tree in the living-room. Mouse chased a jingle bell all over the house.

She, Judy Moody, sang,

"Mele Kalikimaka *is the thing to say*
On a bright Hawaiian Christmas day!"

and *"Have a hula, jula Christmas!*
    It's the best time of the year…"

Dad poked his head into the playroom
off the kitchen. "Pizza will be here any
minute," he said.

"Does Judy have to sing Hawaiian
songs? She knows I want snow."

"Why don't you sing your own carols,
Stink? Like … *Hark! The herald angels sing!"*
Dad belted out.

"Who's this Harold guy everybody's
always singing about anyway?"

"Never mind," said Dad, shaking his
head. Stink put on his snowflake costume
and sang, *"Let it snow! Let it snow!*
Let it snow!"

Just then the doorbell rang. "Pizza!" yelled Stink.

The Moodys sat down to dinner. Judy was the first to grab the pizza table, for her collection. Stink ate all the pineapple off his pizza.

"What a great Christmas show you kids put on this year," said Dad.

"And I didn't have to be a mouse, for once," said Stink.

"Mrs D. was surprised," Mum said.

"Yeah, she kept saying 'mouse', and Stink didn't come out."

"My snowflake got stuck in the door to the stage!" said Stink.

Ding, dong.

"Could that be the pizza man *again*?" Dad asked.

"I'll get it!" called Stink. He raced out of the kitchen and opened the front door. Stink could not believe his eyes. It was Jack Frost, live and in person!

"One more parcel for the Moodys got left behind in my truck," Jack said. "Thought it might be important."

"Wow!" said Stink, taking the parcel. "I never knew the postman came at night!"

Jack Frost laughed. "At this time of year, we work long hours."

"Thanks!" said Stink. "So you think it might snow tonight?"

"Never say never," said Jack. "Might be

making snow angels and having snowball fights yet. Well, gotta go. I still have a lot of work to do!"

"Goodbye, Jack Frost! Have a Holly Jolly Day! I mean a Holly Joliday! I mean a Jolly Holiday!" Stink came back into the kitchen.

"Did you hear that?" he asked his family.

"We heard you wishing somebody a holly *joliday.*" Judy cracked up. "Who *was* it?"

"Jack Frost."

"Not again," said Judy, rolling her eyes.

"Who's Jack Frost?" Mum and Dad asked at the same time.

"You guys don't know who Jack Frost is?" Stink asked.

"He's the new postman," said Judy.

"And he brings snow," Stink added.
"And tonight he brought us a parcel.
Can we open it? Can-we-can-we-can-we?"

"Hmm. No return address on the box,"
said Dad. "Must be from Grandma Lou."

"She already sent fruitcake," said Mum.

"Maybe it's a yule log," said Judy.

"What's a yule log?" asked Stink.

"*Yule* never know!" Judy cracked up
again. "Just open it, Stink!"

Stink ripped the tape off the box. Inside
were two squishy parcels – one marked
for Judy and one for Stink. They tore off
the wrapping paper.

"Mittens!" said Stink. A green pair
for Stink and a red pair for Judy.

"Fa la la la la," said Judy. "I'd rather have fruitcake."

"That's weird," said Stink. "There's still nothing that says who they're from. Just a note saying, 'You'll need these when the snow flies.'"

"Ooh – it's a mystery," said Judy.

"Maybe they're from Jack Frost!" Stink said.

"So now Jack Frost knows how to knit too?" Judy snorted. "Stink, why would the postman give us a present?"

"He's not *just* the postman," said Stink.

∴✳ • ✳ ∴ ✳ ∴

After pizza, Judy and Stink went into the playroom. Stink stared out the window.

Judy decked the halls with Christmas-in-Hawaii stuff – she decorated the blow-up palm tree from the Christmas show with origami surfboards, sailboats and sea horses. She hung a string of pink flamingo lights. Even Mouse got to wear a grass skirt and fake flower *lei.*

Stink pointed to the black sky. "I think I see some clouds!"

"I think you're seeing stars, Kimo," said Judy.

"I wish every one of those stars was a snowflake," said Stink. He sighed. "I hope it snows by midnight. Jack Frost said—"

"Stink," Judy said, craning her neck to look up at the sky, "give it up. No way is it going to snow by midnight."

"Wanna bet?" asked Stink.

"Sure," said Judy. "But if I win, *you* have to eat fruitcake."

"OK, but if I win, you have to help me build a snowman."

"Deal," said Judy.

"Hey, wait just a minute!" said Stink. "How will you know if it snows by midnight? You'll be in bed, sound asleep by then."

"No way," said Judy. "I'm waiting up."

"Cool yule!" said Stink. "Me too!"

8.12 p.m.

"No way am I drinking this!" Stink sniffed the yucky-smelling stuff in his Santa mug.

"It's coffee," said Judy. "That's how you stay awake."

"Coffee! Bluck! I'd rather drink a cup of mud."

"Just try it," Judy told her brother.

"Dad, are we allowed?" asked Stink.

"Go ahead. Try it," said Dad. "It's a special occasion."

"C'mon, Kimo," said Judy. "You go first."

Stink stared into the dark murky liquid. He took a sip. *Bluhhh!* He spat it into the sink. "It tastes like tree bark," said Stink. Dad grinned.

"Tree bark?" said Judy. "There must be other ways to stay awake besides drinking tree bark."

8.43 p.m.

Judy and Stink played all the Christmas CDs they could find. Mum and Dad sang along to "Frosty the Snowman", "Jingle Bell Rock", and "Winter Wonderland". Stink and Judy sang the Grinch theme song at the top of their lungs:

"Your heart is full of unwashed socks;
Your soul is full of gunk, Mr Grinch!
The three words that best describe you
Are as follows, and I quote:
STINK … STANK … STUNK!"

9.15 p.m.

They took turns reading aloud from all the books in the house about snow. *Owl Moon* and *The Snowy Day* and *Snowflake Bentley.* Dad even recited the poem "Stopping by Woods on a Snowy Evening".

"All these snowy books are making me sleepy," said Stink.

"All these snowy books are making me cold," said Judy. "Brrrrr!"

9.23 p.m.

Mum and Dad wrapped more presents.
Judy and Stink played fifty-two-card pickup
about fifty-three times. "No fair. How come
you always get to throw them, and I always
have to pick up all the cards?" asked Stink.

9.36 p.m.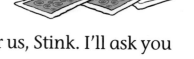

"I have a game for us, Stink. I'll ask you
a question, and you say, 'Freak of nature.'
Ready?"

"Ready, Freddy."

"What's another name for a blizzard in
Virginia?"

"Freak of nature."

"What's your favourite subject at school?"

"Freak of nature."

"What do you call somebody who only wants snow for Christmas?"

"Freak of nature. Hey, wait, that's me!"

"Exactly," said Judy.

9.44 p.m.

"Still no snow," said Stink, reporting from his lookout by the window. He pointed to the thermometer outside. "Hey, good news. It's thirty-eight degrees. The temperature's dropping. It was thirty-*nine* a few minutes ago."

"Well, my temperature's going up every time you check that thing!"

9.52 p.m.

"Kids!" said Dad, poking his head into the playroom. "It's way past your bedtime!"

Mum had ribbon around her neck and a tag stuck to her sweater. "It's past mine too," she said, yawning.

"But it's Christmas Eve!" said Stink.

"We're trying to stay up till midnight," said Judy. "To see if it snows. Can't we just sleep down here in our sleeping bags tonight?"

Mum and Dad gave each other a look. "OK," said Dad. "Mum and I are off to bed. No pillow fights."

"And no more hula dancing. Time to start settling down," said Mum.

"Bah, humbug," said Judy.

She put on her monkey PJs. Stink climbed inside his snowflake sleeping bag. Mum and Dad kissed them good night and turned out the lights. Stink couldn't help closing his eyes.

"Stink, don't flake out on me now," Judy said, plugging the flamingo lights back in. The palm tree twinkled with all the colours of a sunset in Hawaii.

"I'm just resting my eyes," said Stink, yawning.

10.12 p.m.

Judy went to brush her teeth. By the time she came back, Stink was fast asleep. Even Mouse was curled up on a cosy Santa hat.

"Hey, Snoozer," Judy called, but Stink did not wake up. She tried making goofy faces and noises. She tried lifting up his eyelids. She tried tickling him awake with the fuzzy tip of the Santa hat.

Finally, she gave up. Stink was going to be so disappointed that he fell asleep. But he was going to be doubly disappointed when he woke up and there was no snow.

10.27 p.m.

Judy hummed all Twelve Days of Christmas … inside her head.

10.28 p.m.

Judy counted reindeer … inside her head.

10.37 p.m.

Suddenly, in the not-so-silent night, Judy heard something … tapping on the roof. *Reindeer?* She heard something else … tapping at the window. *Jack Frost?* She looked out, when what to her wondering eyes did appear, but…

Rain!

There was only one thing worse than *not* getting snow for Christmas. Getting *rain.* Judy looked over at the sleeping Stink. He was going to be double-triple-quadruply disappointed.

What happened then? Well, in Moodyville they say that Judy Moody's heart grew three sizes that day.

Judy ran to get scissors. Paper. Glitter. Glue. *Snip, snip, snip.* While Stink was asleep all snug on the sofa, Judy made millions of paper snowflakes and stuck them all over the walls, windows and doors.

She sprinkled the teeny-tiny scraps along the windowsill and all across the floor. She even sprinkled Stink while he was sleeping. In the moonlight, the confetti looked like new-fallen snow.

Perfect! *Brain*storms were better than *rain*storms any old day. Now Stink could have a ho-ho, not a ho-hum, Christmas.

Judy could not wait to see Stink's face when he woke up to snow everywhere, even if it was fake. It would be a million times better than watching him eat fruitcake any day.

Judy felt like Old Man Winter. She felt like Santa at the North Pole. She felt like Snow Freak Bentley.

She, Judy Moody, felt like the genuine-and-for-real Jack not-the-postman Frost.

11.57 p.m.

Just before the big hand and the little hand hit twelve, the rain stopped tap, tap, tapping. Judy snuggled down into her cosy sleeping bag. At last, she was ready for some long winter's nap, nap, napping.

Let It Snow

When Stink woke up bright and early
on Christmas morning, he thought he
was dreaming.

"Judy! Wake up! Wake up! Snow! It really
is a white Christmas!"

Judy rolled over. "I know, Stink. It's just
pretend snow. I didn't want you to have
a very muddy Christmas. Or a very moody
one."

"No, Jack Frost was here. For real and
absolute positive. No lie."

"Um-hmmm. He brought us mittens,"

said Judy, snuggling down into her sleeping bag. "It's cold!"

"C'mon, Bed Head." Stink tugged at her sleeping bag. "Just get up and look out the window."

Still wrapped in her sleeping bag, Judy stood up and kangaroo-hopped over to the window. Stink had rubbed a small circle in the frost on the windowpane. Judy and Stink smushed their noses to the glass and peered out. Mouse dashed over to the window too, jingling all the way.

Snow. Real-live, not-fake snow. On houses, trees, rocks, hills and leaves. Everywhere they looked, a blanket of white. A marvellous marshmallow world.

A whipped-cream winter wonderland.

The earth was covered in clean, bright, stellar-dendrite snow. Heaven and nature seemed to sparkle and sing. Joy to the world!

"Snow," Stink breathed. Now he could see why, in Alaska, they had a dozen different words for snow. One word just wasn't good enough.

"A genuine-and-for-real freak of nature!" said Judy.

"It's like being inside a snow globe –
from Vermont!" said Stink. "I wished.
I hoped. I dreamed of a white Christmas,
and my wish came true. Just like Jack Frost
said."

"The world is your snowball, Stink!"
said Judy.

∴ ✳ • ✳ ∙ ✳ ∴

Then Judy and Stink took one look at each
other. Away to the cupboard they flew like
a flash. They pulled on their boots and they
pulled on their hats. They pulled on their
coats and their scarves and their brand-
new, hand-knit mystery mittens.

They held their breath as they opened
the front door.

Judy and Stink stepped outside
into the snowy-blowy, swirly-twirly
winter wonderland.

"Rare!" said Judy.

"Cool yule!" said Stink. "This
is the best holly joliday ever!"